Skateboard Gran

by

Ian MacDonald

Illustrated by Vince Reid

First Published
September 07 in Great Britain by

PUBLISHING

ISBN-10: 1-905637-30-6
ISBN-13: 978-1-905637-30-0

Educational Printing Services Limited
Unit 6, Glenfield Park 2, Northrop Avenue, Blackburn BB1 5QH
Telephone: (01254) 686500   Fax: (01254) 686501
E-mail: enquiries@eprint.co.uk   Website: www.eprint.co.uk

Contents

1   Gran   1

2   Know Your Onions   8

3   Kieran Bates   14

4   "You Can Do It!"   23

5   Just an Old Lady   31

6   Miss Byron   38

7   Digging   45

8   "Look out, Gran!"   53

9   The Skateboard Park   61

10   Wall of Death   70

11   The Winner!   79

12   A Silver Skater   88

Chapter 1
Gran

Everyone said that Tom was sensible.

His hair was sensible.

His shoes were sensible.

His shirt and tie were sensible.

Even his underpants were sensible.

His Gran, on the other hand, was completely bonkers.

"Wheeeeh! Coming through!"

Several schoolboys scattered as a figure on a skateboard clattered towards them. The black skateboard was edged with orange flames. The wheels, the latest aluminium *fast-tracks*, shot sparks onto the pavement. Painted on the top of the board was a vase of flowers.

Planted firmly on the board were two small feet in brown lace-up shoes. From the shoes sprouted two spindly legs wrapped in folds of grey, wrinkled tights. Two bony knees pointed outwards at such an angle that it seemed impossible the skater stayed on the board at all. The figure wore a green woollen coat which flapped open in the wind to reveal a purple, knitted cardigan and a grey skirt. Over one arm dangled a blue, zipped handbag. Clumps of grey hair escaped wildly from under a pink crash helmet.

There was a screech of wheels and the skateboard came careering towards them again. The rider pushed a tiny foot down on the back of the board. She slid the other foot forward. The skateboard flipped up in the air, high above where the boys were sitting. They scrambled for cover, Ben falling back into the prickly, purple bush that he had climbed out of only moments before. Tom glanced up as the old lady sailed over his head.

He wished he hadn't.

"Oh, Gran!" he spluttered.

There were bits of your gran that you didn't want to see.

"Hello boys," said the rider, taking off her helmet.

"Hello, Gran," mumbled Tom.

"What are you lot up to, then?"

"Nothing much," said Tom, looking around anxiously. He was sure that his whole class from school were going to appear around the corner any moment. It wasn't

fair. No one else had to put up with this
sort of thing.

"Anyway, can't stay here all day
gossiping. I've got shopping to do."

Tom gave a sigh of relief.

The old lady tipped up the board and
spun it on her hand. She let it fall forward,
where it did a somersault and landed on the
pavement. Swinging her handbag back over
her arm, she hopped onto the board and
disappeared in the direction of the
vegetable shop.

"Your gran's a nutcase!" said Ben,
climbing out of the shrubbery picking bits of
hedge from his school jumper.

"She ought to be locked up," added
Vijay.

"I know," said Tom, shuffling his feet awkwardly on the pavement.

"Why can't she just knit jumpers and stroke the cat like other old ladies?" said Ben.

"Leave her alone," said Jess. "She's alright, your gran."

"She's not alright. She's completely bonkers," muttered Tom.

Why did his gran have to turn up and embarrass him all the time? Other boys' grans watched the television, or bought you sweets, or ruffled your hair and said how big you'd grown. Why couldn't his gran be like that?

"Come on, look, the library's open," said Tom, glad for the chance to change the subject. "There's a book I'm looking for. I want to see if it's in."

Chapter Two
Know Your Onions

"Do we have to go there?" moaned Vijay.

"Yeah, I don't want my friends seeing me in the library. It's not the coolest place to be, is it?" sniggered Ben.

Tom gave him his best withering stare. "All your friends are here. You haven't got any others!" he said.

"Well, yeah, I know that."

"Are you coming then, or not?"

The four shambled off in the direction of the library. Tom led the way and Jess and Vijay trudged behind, hands thrust deep into their jeans pockets. Ben followed, still tugging at his jumper, leaving an untidy trail of leaves and twigs as he went.

Inside, the library was very quiet.

At the desk a woman glared at them over thick, black-rimmed glasses.

"What's up with 'er?" whispered Jess.

"I dunno," replied Ben. "Perhaps she's scared we might borrow a book or something!"

Vijay wandered off to the non-fiction section and picked a book from the shelf. *How Computers Work.* He sat down at the table and began turning the pages.

Tom ignored the children's book corner and followed the shelves past *Cookery, History, Sport and Travel* until he came to the one he wanted. He lifted the largest book down from the top shelf and placed it on the table beside him.

"How to Grow Vegetables," read Ben. He looked like he had a bad smell under his nose.

"Ssssh! Quiet!" glared a man reading a newspaper at a table nearby.

"Sorry," said Tom.

The man looked up.

Standing on the other side of the shelving was a smartly dressed boy in polished, black shoes. Next to him stood a girl in a short, grey skirt held up by a blue and purple striped tie. Then came a smaller, scruffy looking boy who seemed to be wearing a hedge.

The man looked up just as an earwig appeared in the boy's hair. It looked around, scuttled down to the boy's ear, and lost its balance! The insect plopped onto the man's newspaper where it lay on its back, waving its legs wildly. Then it rolled over, scurried to the edge of the table and fell off onto the floor.

The man sighed, brushed some leaves from his trousers and left.

Jess and Ben sat down on the only two chairs and opened the library book. There was lots of writing. Some of it seemed to be in another language.

"What do you want this for?" asked Jess, frowning.

"I promised the lady next-door I'd find her a book," said Tom, turning to a chapter called, *Know Your Onions*. "She sometimes grows vegetables for the village show. I might get some tips on growing."

"Well, hurry up and get on with it. I don't want to spend all day in here," snorted Jess.

"Cor, look at this!" said Ben, excitedly.

Tom looked over his friend's shoulder. There on the page was a man holding an enormous onion in his arms. It was about the size of a small football. Jess pretended not to be interested, but sneaked a look too.

"Just right," said Tom, "I'll get this."

But, before Tom could pick up the book, another hand reached over, took hold of the page . . . and tore it out.

Chapter Three
Kieran Bates

"Hello, Tom."

It was Kieran Bates.

Kieran was the biggest boy at school.
And he knew it. No one liked him, but
everyone hung around with him. It was the
best way not to get your head punched.

"Shame about the pretty book," Kieran went on, "you really should be more careful."

"But Tom didn't tear it," said Jess. "You did!"

"You trying to get me into trouble, Jessica Fairbrass? 'Cos you know what I'll do to you if you get me into trouble, don't you!"

"Leave her alone," said Ben.

"Yeah, an' what you gonna do about it, Squirt?"

Ben went quiet and looked at his feet. "What about you?" said Kieran, turning on Tom. "You ain't saying nuffing."

"I'll put the book back," said Tom, "no one'll find out."

"There's a good boy." Kieran patted Tom on the head. Then, without warning, he shoved Tom hard in the chest. Taken by surprise, Tom grabbed at a chair and missed. Arms clawing wildly at the air, he fell backwards into the bookshelf. There was a crash as a pile of books came tumbling down, half burying Tom underneath.

"What on earth do you think you're doing?" said a voice.

Tom looked up. He lifted *A Flock of Sheep* from his head. *Queen Victoria* lay on his chest. The librarian with the black glasses was glaring down at him. From where Tom was looking she was the size of a small skyscraper.

"Is this yours?"

In one hand the librarian held a book, and in the other the crumpled, torn page with the football-onion man.

Kieran had gone.

Tom groaned.

"Forty eight pounds!" said Tom, looking glum. "Where am I going to get that kind of money?"

"Don't worry, Tom. We'll think of something," said Jess.

"Maybe you can get people to pay you to do their homework or something," suggested Vijay.

"We'll get Kieran - make him write a confession," said Ben, angrily.

"Yeah, when you're a black-belt in karate," snorted Vijay.

"Besides, Kieran can't write, anyway!" laughed Jess.

"Yeah, thanks, but there's nothing we can do. I'll just have to pay for it myself."

"How are you going to do that?" asked Vijay.

"Pocket money?" suggested Jess.

"Don't get any," said Tom.

"What about a paper round?" said Ben.

"But that would take you . . . " Vijay counted on his fingers . . . "ten weeks at least."

Then, as if things could not get any worse, back came Tom's Gran. She whizzed towards them at high speed. Ben glanced nervously behind him. The purple bush was still there. Just waiting for him. Gran pushed down hard on the back of the board and took off, landing smartly on the low brick wall that surrounded the bushes. Sparks flying everywhere, Gran slid towards them, the board skidding on its footplate, wheels off the ground. She screeched to a halt, the tip of her board almost resting in her grandson's lap.

In her hand Gran was waving a piece of coloured paper.

"Look at this, boys!"

"Er, hum," Jess coughed.

"Sorry, Jess, love, didn't see you there."

Ben climbed back out of the purple bush again, hoping no one had noticed.

"What are you on about, Mrs O?" asked Vijay.

"Well, look here for yourself. It's a competition, see - a skateboard competition, and it's going to be held here in the village."

Tom took the paper from Gran's hand.
He read out loud:

Skateboard Contest

3.00 p.m.

June 25th

Jubilee Fields

"Wow, look," said Jess, peering over Tom's shoulder. "First Prize . . . a new skateboard . . . and fifty pounds cash!"

Chapter Four
"You Can Do It!"

"There's your answer," said Vijay, "enter the skateboard competition and win the money. You'll have enough to pay for the book, and some left over."

"To spend on your mates!" said Ben, putting on his best cheesy grin.

"Yeah, like, two pounds, that's really going to take us all on holiday, isn't it!" said

Jess, raising her eyes to the sky.

"You're all forgetting one thing aren't you?" said Tom.

"What's that?" said Ben.

"I haven't got a skateboard - and I can't skate!"

"That's two things," said Vijay.

"There's no such thing as can't," said Jess. "At least, that's what my teacher says."

"Yeah, well, ever seen a teacher on a skateboard?"

"The competition's not for five weeks yet," said Vijay. "That's loads of time to practise."

"Why don't you use my skateboard -
have a try?" said Gran.

"No thanks. I'm OK, really," spluttered
Tom.

"You'll be OK, look, you can borrow my
knee pads."

Tom groaned as his Gran hitched up her skirts and unstrapped two knee-pads from her wrinkly legs.

"Go on, Tom," Vijay joined in. He could see that Tom was squirming.

"Yeah, go on," said Jess.

"No, I really can't."

"You're not scared are you?" said Ben.

"I . . . I've got homework to do," spluttered Tom.

"A bit of homework can wait. What's more important than having a bit of fun?" said Gran.

Tom couldn't imagine anything worse than having his gran show him up in front of all his friends. It was about as much fun as having a tooth out in assembly.

Gran was now taking off her pink helmet. The skateboard was looking up at Tom like a puppy-dog waiting to be taken for a walk.

"Here put this on," said Gran, placing the helmet on Tom's thick, wiry hair.

"I don't want it!"

"But you can't skateboard without a helmet," said Gran. "It's not safe."

"It's the not-safe bit that worries me," muttered Tom.

It was then that Tom saw Kieran and his gang. They were standing outside the supermarket watching everything. Tom knew that if he was too scared to ride the skateboard he would never hear the last of it.

"Just try, Tom," said Gran, doing up the chin-strap.

"Go, Tom! Go Tom!" said Vijay, waving his hands cheer-leader style.

"Go on, Tom!" said Ben. "You can do it!"

Tom looked in turn at each of their faces. These were his friends. They did everything together. He did not want to let them down. Besides, it would pay for the torn book. There was no other way.

"Yeah, you can do it," said Jess, softly.

Everyone waited.

A pigeon took off and landed on the library roof. It looked down and dropped a white splodge on the pavement below.

"No, I can't," said Tom, taking off the helmet and giving it back to Gran.

Somewhere outside the shops someone was making chicken noises. He didn't have to look. He knew who it was. He knew that Kieran and his gang would be flapping their arms like chickens.

He knew what they thought. That he was a scaredy-cat. Even his friends knew he was too scared to step on a skateboard.

And they were right.

He was.

Chapter Five
Just an Old Lady

"Come back! Come back!"

Tom stopped in his tracks. It was Gran calling. He did not turn around straight away. He first had to wipe his eyes with the back of his hand. He could still hear the gang laughing and squawking, making their stupid chicken noises. What did Gran want now? Why didn't she just leave him alone?

"Tom, come back." This time it was Jess.

Tom turned around. "What? I've said I'm not doin' it. What else do you want?" Tom walked back to where his friends stood.

"You don't have to."

"What do you mean, I don't have to?"

"You don't have to skate," said Gran.

"I've already decided that, haven't I?" said Tom, crossly.

"Just listen to what your gran says," said Jess.

Tom listened.

"I'll do it."

"Do what?"

"The competition!"

"What do you mean, you'll do the competition?"

"Clean your ears out, Tom," said Gran. "I'll do the competition and win the money for you. Jess told me all about the book."

Tom shot Jess a glare. She pulled a face back, but could not help a grin escaping.

"But it's going to be held on a real skateboard park, and everything," said Tom. All the while he was thinking what his mum would say if she found out that Gran was going to be doing leaps off a skateboard ramp at fifty feet. And all because of him. "But you've only ever skated on the precinct, along the pavement, off the walls and benches. Beside you're just a . . . "

"Just an old lady," added Gran.

"I didn't mean . . . "

"I know what you meant. When your grandad was alive he used to say, 'You can do anything if you put your mind to it', and he was right."

Gran was always saying this. It was one of her phrases like, 'It's never too late to learn'. There was no arguing with her when she was in this kind of mood.

"OK then, if you're sure, then I'll help you."

"I thought you weren't going to skate!" said Ben.

"I'm not," said Tom, but I can build you a skateboard park to practise on."

"Wow!" said Jess.

"Great!" said Gran, "when do we start?"

"Straight away," said Tom, "but I want to take this book round to Miss Byron, first. I promised."

Miss Byron lived next door.

Tom often called in there. He would go sometimes at the weekend and find her planting seedlings in the greenhouse; or on her knees pulling weeds out of a flower border; or digging over the heavy clay-soil in her vegetable patch. He had been going there for as long as he could remember.

When they had first moved in Miss Byron had sent a bunch of carrots (other people sent flowers) and Tom's mum had taken to her from the start.

Tom had been allowed to go around sometimes when Mum could keep an eye on him from the kitchen window, and soon he was allowed to go anytime, as long as Mum knew where he was.

Miss Byron was like a favourite aunt to

Tom; not that she would allow such nonsense: "Call me Kate," she said from the start.

"Hello," called Tom. He pushed open the side door . . . and went in.

Chapter Six
Miss Byron

On the kitchen table there was a pile of old
gardening magazines, a roll of garden string,
and a china fruit bowl full of potatoes. Tom
cleared a space, put the book down, and
went out into the garden.

"Hello, Tom."

"What are you doing?" Tom asked.

"What does it look like?" Miss Byron often pretended to be rude, but she was only playing. She used to be a teacher and would not stand for rudeness of any sort.

"It looks like you're making a tent out of sticks," said Tom.

"That's a pretty good guess, my lad," said the old lady. "It's actually called a wigwam, which was a kind of tent the American Indians used."

Miss Byron could recite poetry, tell you the capitals of any country in the world or show you how to tie knots. She seemed to know everything about anything. "If you look down there," she continued, "you'll see some tiny seedlings. They're called sweet peas."

"Can you eat them? I don't like peas much."

"You needn't worry. These are just for show. They grow some very beautiful flowers. But you have to tie them, or the wind will blow them over."

"So that's what the sticks are for?"

"That's right. Now hand me that string will you. I'll hold the canes, and you tie it at the top. Just there."

The two worked busily together until there was a neat row of six wigwams in a straight line along the garden. As they worked Tom told her all about the morning, the torn book, the competition and the skateboard park. She said nothing until he had finished.

"Wait there," she said.

When she came back she was carrying a

spade. Tom could tell it was very old, its
handle wasn't like the spades Tom had seen
in shops, it was long, almost coming to Miss
Byron's shoulders, but the metal blade shone
like new.

"You'll be needing this then," said Miss
Byron.

"For me?"

"It used to belong to my old dad, but it's too big for me. Now take it."

Tom could tell that this was a lie. Kate was big and strong. She looked like she could steal a cow from a field!

"Thanks! I'll look after it."

The next morning Tom was up before anyone was awake. It was Saturday and he wanted to get started on the skateboard park.

He took the spade from under his bed and crept downstairs. Outside it was beginning to get hot already. Tom walked down the winding path to the fence at the

bottom of the garden. Beyond the wooden
fence was a patch of ground under the
trees. It really belonged to Jackson's Farm,
but the farmer had let Tom have it a long
time ago. It was under the trees so there
was no grass to interest the cows that
sometimes grazed in the field.

This muddy patch of waste ground had once held a tree house, later a model village and then a gnome garden . . . with just one gnome. Once, Tom had dug a large hole, covered it with wood and branches, and it had become an underground den. No one knew it was there until the day Dad went to fetch the football and disappeared up to his neck in soil and branches.

But now it was going to be a skateboard park. Tom looked at the flat ground. It looked a big task. He would have to dig slopes and banks and curves and runs, and all out of the hard clay soil under his feet. Well, nothing was going to get done just looking at it. Tom began to dig.

Chapter Seven
Digging

By lunch time Tom was worn out. His arms and legs ached, his back ached and his head ached. His t-shirt was soaked and sweat ran down his face, making spots on the clay ground.

He rested his chin on his spade and looked around. All he could see were holes and piles of dirt, but in his imagination he could still see the skateboard park. It had pathways, ramps and sloping walls to ride up and down. Even so, Tom began to wonder whether it was not all a stupid idea. There had to be other ways to make money. It would probably be a lot easier to get up early every morning and do a paper round.

But he did not want to let Gran down. He had said he would make a skateboard park, and that's what he was going to do. Tom picked up his shovel, wiped the sweat from his forehead and began to dig again.

At four-o-clock his friends arrived.

"What's it s'posed to be?" asked Vijay.

"What a mess!" said Jess.

"Looks like a giant mole's been digging up your garden," said Ben.

"Yeah, thanks a lot," said Tom.

"Only trying to be helpful," said Ben.

"That's a great help," replied Tom, moodily. "If you haven't got anything useful to say, just don't bother, alright."

"We only came to see if you wanted to come down the shops, that's all," said Jess.

"Yeah, if you're not too busy that is," said Vijay.

"What does it look like?" snapped Tom.

"Alright, don't throw your toys out the pushchair," said Ben.

"Come on, you two," said Jess. "Let's leave him alone."

"Yeah, we know when we're not wanted," finished Vijay.

The three friends began to walk away. Tom dropped his spade and called after them. "Hey, don't go. Sorry, I didn't mean all that stuff. I'm just a bit worn out, that's all."

"That's OK," said Jess, turning back. "Are you coming then?"

It was still hot when they arrived at the precinct.

Mr Patel was just bringing in his vegetables, ready for packing up the shop; a few late shoppers were buying something to eat; Mr Liu was putting the sign outside the Chinese take-away.

"What we gonna do then?" said Tom.

"Same as always," said Vijay.

"That's nothing much, then," said Jess.

They all sat down on the sloping wall that ran along the front of the shops. Ben picked up a bread crust that lay on the floor and began tossing bits to a couple of pigeons that were strutting around their feet.

"Sorry, pigeons," he said. "All gone."

Just then he gave a yelp as something hit him on the head. He looked down. It was a bread roll. He picked it up.

"Hey look, it must be the bread fairy," laughed Jess. "She's brought rolls for the pigeons."

Then it was Jess's turn to cry out as something struck her on the ear.

"Oy, what's going on?" she shouted.

Splattered on the pavement was a mouldy looking cabbage. Another bread roll landed, just missing Vijay. And then a tomato caught Tom on the side of the face, showering red juice and pips all over his white t-shirt.

"Who's that?" cried Jess, climbing up on the wall to get a better look.

SMACK!!

A small cardboard carton hit her on the shoulder, spraying milk everywhere.

"Gotcha!" shouted a voice from somewhere outside the supermarket.

No one needed to ask who it was.

They all knew.

Chapter Eight
"Look out, Gran!"

"Sorry, everyone. I didn't see you there."
Kieran lumbered over, a new skateboard
clutched in one meaty hand.

"You did it on purpose," said Ben, angrily.

"Aaw, come on. I was just helping the
supermarket clear out their old stuff. It
was going off anyway." He glanced down at
Tom's shirt. "Oh dear, it looks like some of
it's gone-off on your shirt."

Kieran's gang stood behind him grinning stupidly, enjoying the show.

"How would you like it?" said Jess, picking up the half-empty milk carton.

"Leave it," whispered Vijay, grabbing Jess's arm. He knew that they would come off worse if there was any trouble.

"And what have you been up to?" said Kieran, still staring at Tom. "You look like you've been in a fight already". It was true - he looked a right mess. His shirt, apart from the tomato stains, was covered in sweat and dirt.

"He's been building a skateboard park," said Ben, helpfully.

Tom groaned. That was the last thing

he needed, for Kieran to find out about his secret project. Now it was out.

"Wheee! Coming through!"

Everyone looked up as a figure in a green coat came whizzing towards them. Her arms waved wildly in the air as she fought to keep her balance on the steep slope. Her wheels clattered over the paving with a sound like a speeding train.

Everyone jumped out of the way . . . except Kieran. The skater had been hidden by Tom and his friends. When he saw her it was too late.

WUMPH!

Gran landed in a heap on top of Kieran Bates.

"Sorry, Deary! Are you alright? I hope I haven't broken anything," said Gran getting to her feet.

"You silly old boot!" spat Kieran, angrily.

"That's no way to speak to an old lady," said Gran. "Has no one ever taught you any manners?"

"You're nuts!"

"Maybe I am," said Gran cheerily, "but at least I'm not sitting in a puddle of milk."

Kieran looked down at his soaked jeans. "I'll get you for this!" he snarled.

"You'll have to catch me first," winked Gran.

Gran picked up her skateboard and hopped on. She pushed hard on the ground

with her trailing foot, and sped off across
the pavement. Kieran struggled to his feet
and put down his skateboard. He pushed off
hard and hurtled off towards the old lady,
leaving a snail-trail of white milk-splodges
behind him.

Gran now turned her board and sped up the sloping wall that ran along the edge of the bushes. Kieran followed. Now he was gaining on the old lady. But Gran saw him coming, and put on a burst of speed, zig-zagging as she went.

Kieran pushed harder on the ground and began to catch up.

Gran flipped her board into the air, skidded along a bench and clattered back to the pavement. But this time Kieran turned and went the other way.

"Look out, Gran!" shouted Tom.

Gran had not noticed Kieran swing his skateboard around. He was now coming towards her, head on. If one of them did not turn away they were certain to crash.

Kieran was much bigger than the little old lady; she would come off worse.

At the last second, Gran slammed her foot on the back of the board, spun high into the air, screeched down the metal handrail, and back to the ground.

It all happened too quickly for Kieran. He was so busy watching Gran that he had not noticed that he had just run out of wall. With a splintering sound, the skateboard thumped into the raised brick at the end of the slope. With a cry of surprise Kieran flew through the air . . . and landed in a heap in the bushes.

Gran picked up the boy's baseball cap, shook off some drops of milk, and tossed it to him.

"See you at the competition, sonny!"

Chapter Nine
The Skateboard Park

It was finished.

The skateboard park had taken every hour of the first three weeks of the summer holiday. But, since it was finished, Gran had been practising daily. Now, with only two days left until the competition, she was on good form.

"It's amazing," laughed Jess.

"It's really ace, man," smiled Vijay.

"Something special!" breathed Ben.

"It's not bad, is it?" said Tom, leaning on his spade.

In front of them a winding path curved away to little tracks, climbs, walls and steep jumps. At the end two perfectly curved walls faced each other, towering above their heads.

"Whooopeee!"

The four friends looked up as a skater in flying skirt whizzed over their heads, and bounced off a low, curved wall. There she spun around, took off again and landed on a snaking path. The rider leaned over, making the skateboard zig-zag sideways as she came towards them. Finally, with a flourish, she tipped the board back and skidded to a halt inches from where they were standing.

"Ride it, Skater!" shouted Ben.

"Knock 'em out, Mrs Gran," yelled Vijay.

"Go, go, Mrs O," whooped Jess.

"Competition's good as won," said Gran, dusting off her shoes. "That Kieran Whatsisname won't stand a chance."

"How about going down the Jubilee?" said Vijay. "They're just finishing the jumps for the competition."

"Maybe we can eye up the opposition while we're there," said Ben.

"Yeah, OK," agreed Tom. "You coming, Gran?"

"You go on, I'm just going to finish my practice session," said Gran. "I'll see you later."

"Bye, Gran."

"See you, Mrs O."

Most days at the Jubilee Fields you would see a few dog walkers; maybe a game of football with jumpers for posts; perhaps a straggle of teenagers lolling on the swings. But today Jubilee Fields was a giant skateboard park.

It was impressive. Great sheets of wooden board were held up on metal

scaffolding. There were tracks and jumps
and loops, and two great wooden walls which
curved up towards the sky. From this side
of the field it looked a bit like a giant roller
coaster.

Three men in black t-shirts were
tightening bolts with spanners; two others in

yellow safety-jackets stood talking, clipboards in hands.

Everywhere there were banners and flags announcing the competition tomorrow.

"Wow!" said Jess.

"Neat!" said Vijay.

"Storming!" said Ben.

"It's a track just made for . . . "

". . . Skateboard Gran!" finished Jess, and she leaned over and squeezed her friend's arm. Tom blushed.

All around the orange fencing stood children clutching skateboards. They looked like surfers waiting for a big wave.

Tom and the others wandered around for a while watching as the workmen put the final touches to the park. After a while there was nothing much else to see and they began to wander back.

On the way home Tom ran through the crowd of faces in his mind's eye. There was Danny and Nathan from his own class; Jezz Wickham the roller-blade champion; Tanya Metcalf, the school show-off, and several boys from the football team. One face was missing.

"Where was Kieran?" asked Tom.

"What are you on about?" said Ben, looking puzzled.

"Who cares!" said Vijay.

"No, but everyone else who's likely to be in the competition was there."

"What's it matter?" said Jess.

"Who wants to see his ugly face, anyway," joined in Ben. "He was probably somewhere stuffing a burger into his big mouth."

Everyone laughed. Except Tom.

"Hey, Tom, has your mum been shrinking your t-shirts," said Jess, poking at a glimpse of stomach.

"I dunno," said Tom, "maybe she's got a new washing powder, or something."

"His shirts haven't shrunk," said Vijay, "it's all that digging! Tom just got muscles!"

But Tom wasn't listening. They had arrived back and now he was staring at his skateboard park.

Or what was left of it!

Everywhere he looked there were broken bits of board and poles scattered across the ground. And it looked like a bulldozer had flattened the mud ramps.

It was completely wrecked.

Chapter Ten
Wall of Death

"Something terrible's happened."

It was Tom's mum. She ran down the path and stood next to her son.

"It's awful!" she said again, panting for breath.

"I know," said Tom flatly. "I can see it."

"No, no, not that. It's your gran, she's in hospital. She fell off that stupid skateboard thing. She's broken her leg!"

✧ ✧ ✧

When they arrived at the hospital Gran was sitting up in bed. A woman in a white coat was standing at her bedside looking at a clipboard.

"Hello, boys!" called Gran, when she saw them.

"And me, Gran!"

"Oh, yes, of course, Jess, love. I count you as one of the boys."

"What have you been doing, Gran?" said Tom, staring at the plaster cast on Gran's leg.

"Oh, it's nothing. Just a little accident, that's all," said Gran.

"More than a little accident, I'd say," said the doctor, putting her pen in her top pocket.

"Oh, stuff and nonsense!"

"But it's all my fault," stammered Tom.

"I should never have built that skateboard park."

"What are you on about, Tom? You do talk stupid sometimes. I didn't do it on the skateboard park. I fell off a wall on the way to the precinct. I just thought I'd practise my air-hanger . . . and I just didn't hang!"

"Well, you could have been very badly hurt. A woman of your age should know better," said the doctor. "No more skateboarding for you, I'm afraid."

"But!"

"No buts. No skateboarding. Not ever!"

Gran turned to Tom. "Well, that's it. You'll just have to go in my place, Tom."

"But!"

"No buts!" said Gran, winking at Jess. "You're in the competition. Here's your entry-ticket."

Tom balanced at the top of the starting ramp and glanced down at his skateboard.

It was an Emerson-Lightning: the best. Its narrow, tapered sides were shaped for extra speed; the twin-mounted wheels were alloy speed-tracks; between his feet was painted a vase of flowers.

Suddenly this seemed a really bad idea. But he had do it, not just for the money, but for Gran.

Just as well he had been secretly practising on his own skateboard park when

no one was around.

"Ready, Seven?"

Tom nodded. It was his number.

There had been twenty three other skaters before him; now there were just two left: Tom, and then Kieran Bates.

The scoring system was complicated. The time around the course scored up to ten points and another ten could be added for style over the jumps. Penalty points were taken away for falls. Not completing the course scored zero. The score to beat was 17.9, by Craig Wickham, the roller-blade champion from class seven. Tom also knew he had to set a high enough score to push Kieran to the limit.

Now it was time.

The hooter sounded and Tom glanced up to see the digital clock flick into motion. He pushed off on his board. It felt like falling over the edge of a cliff. The wind hummed in his ears as he dropped at high speed and came to the first bend. Leaning over, hands held wide for balance, Tom took the first turn easily.

In and out of the slalom gates and on to the first jump. Take the jump safely and go for speed . . . or perform his first trick for style-points?

Too late to think about it.

Tom pushed down on the back of the board as he hit the slope. Tipping the board upward, he leaned his head to the right. Body and board turned together, making a circle in the air. The ground rushed to meet him and he bent his legs to take the shock. The board bounced a little but did not lose speed. The air-spin must have gained him valuable style-marks.

There was a whoop from the crowd as he made his landing, and Tom sped on towards the inclined wall. He put his trailing foot down, scooting against the ground to pick up speed again. There was the wall. He leaned over and took the slope high, snaking his board up and down the slope. This would lose a fraction of a second in time, but earn more style marks again.

Now just the finish:

The Wall of Death.

The run had gone well, he knew. The crowd sensed it too. Just the wall . . . and it would be over.

Chapter Eleven
The Winner!

Tom looked for the steepest downhill slope
to pick up as much speed as he could.
He whizzed into the first bank, looped all
the way to the top and arched the board
around. The board seemed to stand still in
the air as it took off. It turned and
dropped back towards the earth. No one
could tell whether the rider's wheels were
back on the wall, or whether he was skating
on the air; his touchdown was almost silent.

The final jump and it was finished.

Tom saw the top of the wall coming towards him. He braced himself for his final leap.

He had already planned how he would finish; he saw the double back-flip in his imagination. He reached forward to grasp the front of the board. As he did so he felt the board wobble under his feet. Just once. But that was enough. Desperately he tried to regain his balance, but he was already at the top of the wall.

He took off into the air.

Tom stuck out one hand to get hold of the board . . . and missed. Silently, as if in slow motion, the board turned gracefully in the air.

But there was no skater on board. Tom
flailed his arms in the air for a moment . . .
and landed hard on the ledge at the top of
the wall. His skateboard went sailing back
down without him. There it climbed the
opposite slope, rolled back down again, and
came to rest.

There was a half-hearted ripple of applause from the crowd, a few giggles behind hands.

Tom slipped off the wall and slid down to collect his skateboard.

Looking up, he could see the next rider stepping up to the start. And, even from this distance, he could tell that Kieran was grinning.

He could not bear to watch.

Tom ducked his head under the scaffolding and walked a little way to the shadow of the skateboard ramps and jumps. He found a grassy bank at the far end of the track and sat down miserably. He did not want to see anyone or speak to anyone, not even his friends.

Everything had gone wrong.

He looked up at the criss-cross of metal scaffold poles. A spider was trying to catch hold of a piece of scaffolding to make a web. It swung back and forward trying to get a hold of the pole on the other side.

Tom watched, barely interested, trying to forget the events of the last five minutes. But his mind would not let go. In his head he could see the run begin again, the slopes speeding away under his board, the jumps, the spins, the landings. And then the final wall coming up to meet him.

Something had made him lose his balance. What was it?

Tom looked again at the spider. It swung this way and that but could not get a grip on the red scaffold. Something was stopping it. Tom looked harder.

At the top of one of the poles there was a hole where there should have been a bolt. There it was on the floor. A gust of wind blew and the pole shook. The spider swung and missed again.

Tom stood up and looked above his head. Yes, this was the place where he had tried to make his final jump. The loose pole must have made the wall shake, and that was enough for him to lose his balance.

The wind blew hard again. Another bolt slipped away from the scaffold, and dropped to the grass at his feet. Tom leapt up and shook the scaffold hard. Several bolts rattled. Here the whole frame was loose. It had not been checked properly. The non-stop pounding of the skaters had worked the

bolts free. And there was one rider still to
go.

Tom stood up and raced along to the
start.

"Stop! Stop!"

The crowd cheered loudly as the hooter
sounded for the start.

"Come back! Stop the race!"

But no one heard. They were all too
busy cheering. Everyone knew that a good
score now would see Kieran Bates lift the
prize.

"Oh, no," groaned Tom.

He pushed through the crowds and
began to run back, ducking under the

scaffolding as he went. He could hear the clatter of the board over his head as Kieran sped around the track. He could picture the moves and jumps as he listened to the sounds the skateboard made above him: now running at speed, now turning the corner, now making a jump. Soon he would be nearing the final bend . . . and the Wall-of-Death.

Tom heard the rider above him start his approach.

"Must get there first . . . "

Breathing hard, Tom reached the place where he had seen the spider. He reached up and gripped the two longest red poles. The muscles bulged under his t-shirt. Above him there was a moment's quiet. Kieran had made a perfect leap in to the air. Tom held on tight and waited. He felt as if his arms were going to burst. And then, with a noisy clatter of wheels, the boards shuddered as the skater landed.

A loud cheer went up.

The Winner!

Kieran Bates.

Chapter Twelve
A Silver Skater

"Oi, you, what's your game?"

Tom blinked his eyes at the shape coming towards him.

"What do you think you're doing?"

Tom looked up. He was still holding tightly to the scaffolding. His arms hurt and his t-shirt was wet with sweat.

The man in the yellow jacket looked down at the boy's feet. There were several metal bolts lying on the ground. It only took him a few seconds to work out what had happened.

"Hold on! Don't move, son. I'm going to get help."

Everyone at the finish line was cheering loudly.

A woman in a white suit was holding a trophy in the shape of a silver skater. In her other hand she held a brown envelope.

"The clear winner with a score of 19 points is . . . "

"Stop!"

The woman in white stopped.

Up onto the platform came a red faced man in a yellow jacket. Behind him, in a sweaty t-shirt one-size too small, was a lanky boy with wiry hair. Some of the crowd recognised Tom. There was some pointing and a few whispers behind hands.

"Look at this," said the man in the yellow jacket, and he held out a handful of rusty bolts. "If it wasn't for this boy," said the race supervisor, "there could have been a terrible accident." Turning to Kieran he added, "You just had a lucky escape, young man."

Kieran looked at the bolts and then at Tom.

He gulped. And then, without a word, he took the envelope and the silver statue

and handed them both to Tom.

"Go Tom! Go Tom!" shouted a girl's voice from the crowd.

And everyone began to clap.

"Well, I'm glad that's all over," said Tom as he pushed through the swing doors marked, Anderson Ward. "Still, the trophy will look good on Gran's windowsill."

"You're not giving it away after all that, are you?" said Vijay.

"You must be bonkers," said Ben.

"No, he's very sensible, aren't you Tom," said Jess, grinning. "Anyway, I think Gran will love the silver skateboarder. It'll look just right next to her china cats."

"Well, she deserves it. She won't ever win one now. She's not ever going to skate again, is she?"

"That's what you think!" laughed a nurse, appearing from Gran's room.

"What do you mean?" said Tom.

"See for yourself," smiled the nurse.

"Wheeeeh!" came a voice they all knew.

"Gran!" shouted Tom, and rushed through the swing doors.

"Tom, my boy. Look! I'm supreme Skateboard Champion of the world."

Tom stared, his eyes wide.

Jess, Vijay and Ben stumbled into the room and looked.

"This is really great. I haven't been this good since I did a double back-flip off the library wall."

The four friends watched as a skateboarder sailed across the computer screen.

Gran flipped the joystick and the skater jumped up onto a high wall. There the skater, in a shiny pink helmet, did a

double somersault and swooped back to the
ground.

"Gran!" sighed Tom. "You're completely
bonkers!"

Also available from

PUBLISHING

Alien Teeth   *(Humorous Science Fiction)*
Ian MacDonald   ISBN 978 1 905637 32 2

Eyeball Soup   *(Science Fiction)*
Ian MacDonald   ISBN 978 1 904904 59 5

Chip McGraw   *(Cowboy Mystery)*
Ian MacDonald   ISBN 978 1 905637 08 9

Close Call   *(Mystery - Interest age 12+)*
Sandra Glover   ISBN 978 1 905 637 07 2

Beastly Things in the Barn   *(Humorous)*
Sandra Glover   ISBN 978 1 904904 96 0
www.sandraglover.co.uk

Cracking Up   *(Humorous)*
Sandra Glover   ISBN 978 1 904904 86 1

Deadline   *(Adventure)*
Sandra Glover   ISBN 978 1 904904 30 4

The Crash   *(Mystery)*
Sandra Glover   ISBN 978 1 905637 29 4

The Owlers   *(Adventure)*
Stephanie Baudet   ISBN 978 1 904904 87 8

The Curse of the Full Moon *(Mystery)*
Stephanie Baudet   ISBN 978 1 904904 11 3

A Marrow Escape *(Adventure)*
Stephanie Baudet   ISBN 1 900818 82 5

The One That Got Away *(Humorous)*
Stephanie Baudet   ISBN 1 900818 87 6

The Haunted Windmill *(Mystery)*
Margaret Nash   ISBN 978 1 904904 22 9

Trevor's Trousers *(Humorous)*
David Webb   ISBN 978 1 904904 19

The Library Ghost *(Mystery)*
David Webb   ISBN 978 1 904374 66

Dinosaur Day *(Adventure)*
David Webb   ISBN 978 1 904374 67 1

There's No Such Thing As An Alien *(Science Fiction)*
David Webb   ISBN 1 900818 66 3

Laura's Game *(Football)*
David Webb   ISBN 1 900818 61 2

Grandma's Teeth *(Humorous)*
David Webb   ISBN 978 1 905637 20 1

Snakes Legs and Cows Eggs *(Humorous)*
Adam Bushnell   ISBN 978 1 905637 21 8

Order online @ **www.eprint.co.uk**